RETROWAVE 2067

A Virtual Reality Adventure

BLAKE LONGDON

Sydney, Australia
www.ausxippublishing.com

Edited: Rosa Alonso
Cover Design: Mary D. Brooks
Produced by: AUSXIP Publishing

ISBN: 978-0-6481042-8-5

Printed in the United States

AUSXIP Publishing
Sydney, Australia
www.ausxippublishing.com

DEDICATION

I dedicate this book to all of my friends, family, and partners I have made throughout my lifetime, they have helped me through hard times, and have pulled me out of ditches I dug myself into, I hope I can only do the same, or better for them in the future.

ACKNOWLEDGEMENTS

Rosa Alonso: A true power player in editing, formatting, and writing this and making all this possible, incredible amounts of props to her.

Mary D. Brooks: The Mastermind behind all this happening, she taught me to do this and inspired me to finish this. I wouldn't be writing this if we hadn't met.

Christine Longdon: Very elemental in making this possible and a huge inspiration for me.

Russ Longdon: My dad was very helpful in this entire process, he gave me character inspiration and helped build the story, tons of thanks to him.

Finally, thank you to my beta-readers for your feedback and support! It takes a village to birth a story.

1
THE RED, CYBERNETIC SUN

So, I have no idea if anyone is alive to read this, but if anyone is outside the S.M.V., then I have quite a story for you. Allow me to introduce myself. My name is Ekalb Dar. I was born on June 4th, 1965, and I was your average Atari-playing, cassette-breaking, trouble-causing, 15-year-old. I used to live on 607th street SW, in Miami, Florida. Before I came here, to the S.M.V., I watched an ad on TV about this technological breakthrough and how it would affect our everyday lives. Humans and technology could finally be integrated into one another, vacations would now cost almost nothing, waiting would be a thing of the past, and entertainment would find a whole new outlet.

This was called the S.M.V., which stands for "Simulated Mind Vacation." It sounds like a robotic savior, I know, but it was different. It was created by a Japanese tech company named "Nami" that, despite the political unease and undeclared war between the U.S. and its allies against the Soviet Union, had the abilities and the funds to produce anything, no matter the cost.

Nami proved their impressive capability when they created the "self-recharging battery," which allowed batteries to have almost limitless power, thus solving the world's small power crisis. Now Nami had built the S.M.V., and everyone wanted to try it.

I was chosen out of a hundred candidates to be a test subject during the early stages. The tests we had to go through in order to even qualify for the S.M.V. were crazy. We had to stay up late working on equations, science questions and so on. I was described as the "perfect candidate" by one Nami scientist. I don't know if this was because I was different from everyone else, or if I had something special that Nami wanted. They never told me, but I was too excited to even care. I was in every magazine, newspaper, and on every TV screen in the world. I even got my own TIME magazine cover! How about that?

The lead engineer working on this project explained it all to me. Here's how it works: the S.M.V. is a virtual reality world that runs off hundreds of thousands of high-power computers that process and create a virtual landscape rapidly, even faster than light. One Nami scientist told me that if they had engineered it correctly, I shouldn't feel anything until I was inside the S.M.V., and I shouldn't feel any different there than I did in the real world, apart from the absence of hunger.

The room housing the S.M.V. looked like a surgical operating theater with a giant camera on the ceiling and a white metal table underneath. Surrounding the theater were hundreds of rows of computers. They had me sit down, they put a weird hat-type thing on my head, and they strapped it down to my chin. It was comfortable in spite of being made entirely out of metal.

I waited a total of three minutes before the S.M.V. began to boot up with a loud whirring sound and then a quiet humming sound. Yes, I was counting. They explained that they had to load up the simulation and make sure everything was in working order. They began to count down from 10, and then, all of a sudden, there was a bright flash and everything went dark.

I woke up, still in the same clothes as I had on before, but there were no buildings, no walls…nothing but a bright, neon sun. The ground underneath had turned into a hot pink grid, and the sky was a mix of purple and black swirling. Dark mountains with blue outlines rose up on the horizon. I didn't know how big this virtual world was, but I planned to see it all and then I'd get back to reality, because I knew I'd miss my friends. The scientist at Nami was right though--I felt the same as I had before.

2
THE CYBER SHORES

I did some walking, and I saw that the S.M.V. cycled through day and night. I liked it when the sun set, and nighttime was just as cool--the grid glowed a hot neon pink and the stars shone bright. I remembered I had a pack of gum, even though the letter from Nami told me not to bring any food with me. I finished the gum that night while I watched the stars. I felt like I needed to eat something, but I didn't physically feel hungry; just mentally. I didn't eat the gum, of course. It tasted really old, kind of hard, and I didn't think Nami would care that I spat it out inside their multi-billion-dollar machine, right?

I discovered a beachhead leading out to a coastline that seemed to go on infinitely. The sand looked like little glowing dots, and the water was dark and silent, and it felt quite warm when I touched it. I messed around in it; it reminded me of when I used to hang out with my friend Tony down at the beach in Miami. I wondered if he even knew where I was.

I figured that this ocean was unfinished land that the S.M.V.

never rendered but created an ocean instead. I tried drinking the water and it tasted like the smell of hot electronics, if that makes any sense. It turned out that the sand was a ton of microscopic Space Invaders! I lined a bunch of them up to make a model of the game. It took a while and I couldn't really see them unless I was looking hard, but I managed. I tried making a sandcastle that fell over as soon as I erected it.

The S.M.V. was very advanced, especially being in its testing stage. I thought I might try drowning myself to see if anything happened. I know it sounds morbid, but since I didn't seem to get tired, it was worth a shot, right?

3
LODESTAR

I tried drowning myself like I said I would in my last log. I woke up in a dark room. There was an Apple computer sitting on a table, and it turned on when I walked up to it. I was confused about what to do, and then a blank text box appeared on the bright, humming, fluorescent screen. It said, "Please, enter valid password." I started entering random words, such as "wave" or "cassette," and, after a while, I got frustrated and gave up.

I suddenly saw a door behind me. I opened it and a bright, almost blinding light blasted out of it. I was feeling adventure-esque, so I entered it and found myself right back at the beach where I had been before. I had a splitting headache and rested a bit before getting up and walking further down the beach. I noticed the door was gone, nada, nothing there…it gave me a weird tingly feeling.

A few hours later, I found a white, shiny, metal panel that looked like it had been blown off something and had the word "Lodestar" on the side. I examined it closely and saw a small satchel on the back. I opened it and found a glowing compass that was pointing West, even though the neon red sun was rising to my left, which was South. It was weird, but I figured that I should follow the compass until I came to something. After all, I had all the time in the S.M.V., at least until the virtual sun set. I liked running because my shoes made a nice squeaking sound. I wished I had my skateboard though—we had so many adventures together! I went to Hollywood with it, to the Bahamas, and even to New York! I had brought my dad's Ray-Bans and that was a good memory to have with me. He got them from when he used to fly cargo. His job sounds so cool! I wanted to become a fighter pilot when I got older because I loved learning about jets and other airplanes and about the gear they use.

4

THE CITY OF ILLUMINI

I had been following the compass for a while when I saw tall, rectangular structures far off into the distance; it almost looked like a city. It seemed to be where the compass was pointing, and I thought it would take me roughly two hours to get there. I wondered if there was any other entity here apart from myself. I wanted to believe so, but the scientist at Nami said that I was the first one to enter the S.M.V. mainframe. I started to suspect that he hadn't told the truth when I saw the buildings in the distance. I was almost there; I could hear sounds coming from the city, like beeping and people talking. I was unsure if this was a glitch in the system or if there were actually people around here too.

I reached a tall, jet-black metal barrier. I banged on it and I heard a voice from inside yell, "Yeah, yeah, let me open it." Within seconds, the doors swiftly swung open and a healthy, normal looking man wearing a mechanic's jumpsuit, roughly in his thirties and about my dad's height, walked out and gave me a welcoming smile. I felt a rush of excitement and choked up a bit from relief. He asked me if I was alright and I replied I was cool. We walked into a small booth a few feet from the towering door. I saw a holographic display shine up from the booth that read, "Welcome to Illumini, traveler! We hope that you enjoy your stay here. There will be a worker with you shortly to help you sign in!"

The man handed me a shiny black board with the words "Please, sign on the line below" in neon blue. I signed my name with a small pen-shaped device that was attached to the side of the board. I handed it back to the man and he said, "Ekalb? Huh, you're new here? Oh, well, you don't have an ID band yet, so let me get you one."

He grabbed what looked like a small wristwatch, plugged it into a terminal that was sitting next to him, and typed my name, age, weight, and height. I don't know how he figured all that out just by looking at me, but I looked down to fix my jacket and saw a small little robotic bug crawling off my pants and into the terminal the man was working at. I tried to warn him that a bug had just walked into a hole in his computer, but he shushed me as soon as I opened my mouth. After a good five minutes of waiting, he gave me my wrist band and told me that it was crucial to wear it at all times if I wanted to stay in Illumini. Then he closed the gates and began to walk away. I asked him if there was anything I should know before I went into the city, and he said I'd figure everything out in time.

After exiting the gate area, I walked into a busy, crowded street--it looked like a marketplace that you would find in Egypt or something. There were cars that looked like the Lamborghini Countach, and some people wore shutter shades that gave off light and they all had the same ID bands as me. This place was cool, yet so weird at the same time. I had to find somewhere to sleep.

5

THE ADMIN

That night I slept at a really nice hotel not too far from where I entered Illumini. It was an upscale luxury hotel: nice beds with fluffy sheets and great customer service. They said that it was free for people who were new to the city. The next morning, I decided to walk around for a while and check out the marketplace. I was confronted by a bald man who seemed to be in his sixties. He wore robes and had transparent pupils; he looked blind but acted like he wasn't. He asked me how long I had been in the city, and I explained that I had been in the S.M.V. for a couple of days (from what I could tell), and in Illumini for less than a day. His soulless, transparent eyes widened, and he muttered something under his breath, grabbed me by the arm and pulled me into a market stand. I yelled "HEY!" as loud as possible, but people looked away as if nothing had happened.

I opened my mouth to yell again but he covered it as soon as air even escaped. He pulled out a walkie-talkie and mumbled something to someone over the radio. I tried not to panic about what was going to happen next, but the fact he knew something about me that was so important that he just had to call someone else made my mind move at a ludicrous speed, jumping from thought to thought and scenario to scenario.

We waited two or three minutes before I saw a black, shaded out Ferrari 308 GTBi drive up outside, and the old man hustled me into the vehicle like someone else was going to come grab me. I tried to get my arm out of his firm grip, but he held even tighter and tighter the more I pulled! He shoved me into the passenger seat and closed the door. Then he walked over to the driver side door and whispered something to the driver about taking me to the "administrator" with the utmost haste.

The window closed and we started driving away to a massive tower called "The Keeper," according to a sign written in bright pink neon. The driver looked like Elvis Presley, except his sideburns didn't go down his cheeks. He was wearing aviator sunglasses and had a freakishly well-defined jawline. I asked him about the tower and all he said was that it was "home." I was so confused. Whose home did he mean? His? My new home?

Once we arrived, he pulled up to the curb leading up to the entrance and told me to get out when he opened the door. I did, not wanting to cause any more trouble than I seemed to have already caused. We walked up to automatic sliding glass doors and we were greeted by a woman in her twenties with white hair in a blue outfit who was sitting behind a reception desk with three file cabinets behind her. She appeared to be the secretary. The driver handed her a card that was roughly the size of a debit card. The woman inspected it thoroughly and handed it back to him.

He looked at me and said, "Come on; the elevator ride is going to be long."

We walked down a long, narrow hallway with doors on each side from the start to the end. He called an elevator, and when the doors opened, he pressed a button labeled "Admin." There was no music playing at all; just the humming of the elevator and the sound of the driver breathing.

Once we reached the top floor, we walked into a large study.

At the other side of the room there was a woman sitting at a desk. She looked almost like the female version of Michael Jackson--kind of scary. The tall walls on our left and right had nothing on them. There was a sofa and some chairs on one side of the room, and a large, king-size bed on the other. I was kind of puzzled about what this place was. When we reached the desk, the woman looked up at the driver and nodded. He walked back to the elevator and left. I looked around the room while I was waiting for the woman to say something.

"Ekalb?" She asked.

"Oh, yes, ma'am?"

She gave me a friendly smile. "Do you know why you are here?"

"I am a test subject for the S.M.V. project and the first person to have ever tried it."

She looked surprised. "I thought the same thing until others began to show up here."

"What do you mean?"

"I mean that I was a test subject for the S.M.V. just like you. I waited for years and years before I finally met the man who drove you here. He was the first contact I had since my arrival. He and I built this city together from nothing. We learned how to use the S.M.V. to create buildings, cars, comforts, and even people! Almost everyone you've seen here isn't real, but instead a fracture of the S.M.V. that we learned to make sentient. Fracture meaning that we scraped off loose data from inside the S.M.V. and formed it into something new. We taught them how to live and how to experience new things."

"Wow," I said under my breath. "So Nami sent other people here before me?"

"Yes," she said.

"I want to get out though. I want to go back to my life."

"We all do, and the fact that you are here means that Nami hasn't abandoned the S.M.V. project, so there is still a chance to get out."

"How? Is there anything I can do to help?"

"No, not now at least. I must contemplate how and when there might be a way out, a hole in the system. For now, you must rest. We will continue talking about this tomorrow."

"Fine," I huffed. She showed me to a bedroom that she said would be mine until I left. It was quite spacious and nice. It had dim-blue lighting that was coming from an unknown place in the room. And there was a white queen-sized bed with clean, silk sheets and a long body pillow with a palm-bush plant next to it. In the front of the room there were a Philips TV, a cassette tape player, and a Betamax movie player. A wide glass window took up a large portion of the room and overlooked the entire city--it was like any other city in the real world, constantly alive, always moving, never sleeping. I turned to ask the woman what her name was, but she had left without making a sound. I figured that was my cue to go to bed, so I took full advantage of it, as I was exhausted.

6
CYPHPRUS

I generally sleep well, but I couldn't seem to sleep at all that night. I would close my eyes and nothing, I would try a new sleeping position every fifteen minutes, I tried on my back, my front, my side, my other side, and none of it worked. This was probably because I was deep in thought about what the woman had said about her being here before me, and how I somehow trusted her more than anyone else in this city. I eventually gave up and decided to get up.

I stumbled and fumbled around in the cold, dry darkness, and eventually made my way to the door. It felt locked at first, but I carefully opened it, and a gust of cold air met my face and made me shiver. My shoes made no noise...who knew Vans could be so quiet? I crept through her room, trying to be as stealthy as possible. I first looked around for a staircase, but of course there wasn't one, because that would be logical! I made my way to the elevator and I pressed the "down" button. The elevator arrived faster than I expected, and I figured it had come from a level other than the ground floor. Me being me, I thought that there was no problem at all. Then it hit me: there was probably someone in the elevator.

I felt a hot wave of adrenaline rush over my body. I ran over to a nearby pillar and hid behind it. I was praying my insanely loud heartbeat wouldn't betray my position. I peered out and saw the same woman from before and two guys, big guys, walking behind her. They both had Uzis trained on her lower back and were wearing blue sports jackets with the sleeves rolled up and gray slacks with brown leather shoes and silver pilot-style glasses. They looked tough, so I decided to stay hidden. I watched as they escorted her over to her desk and shoved her into her seat. The one on the right told her something that I couldn't hear, and she reached into her desk and pulled out a floppy disc and handed it to the man, who snatched it out of her hand with excessive force. They both holstered their Uzis and walked towards the elevator and left. I looked over to the woman and saw she was sitting there quietly, looking out over the city. I decided to go back to my room unnoticed and try to forget what I had seen. I slowly snaked my way across the room and over to my room door. I was pretty sure she had seen me, because I felt an eerie presence on me while I was moving. I lay down, closed my eyes, and finally fell asleep after that terrible night.

7
POSSIBILITY

I woke up to the same digital sun that had plagued me every day since I first arrived in the S.M.V.. I couldn't tell you what time it was, mainly because there was a noticeable lack of clocks around the room, but if I had to guess, I'd say around 12 pm or so. I lay in bed for a good ten minutes before I got up ready to leave. I turned the door handle, but it wouldn't budge. I turned it harder, yet it wouldn't turn. I started throwing myself into the door, attempting to break free of my luxurious prison. During my escape attempt, I broke the lock and figured that I had ruined my chances to get out.

I sat up against a wall contemplating what I had just done and came up with a horrific but strangely brilliant idea--I'd break the bedroom window and jump out. The rational side of me thought this was complete madness, but I figured I had no other choice, so I grabbed the chair at the desk on the other side of the room and threw it with all my might, smashing the window into thousands of pieces. I looked down and saw the death-defying fall to the city streets. I stood there for a second and then hyped myself up to the point where I ran and jumped without even thinking. I opened my eyes and saw the ground getting closer and closer to me without slowing or stopping. I closed my eyes and then everything was silent. No voices, no cars driving, nothing. Just eerie nothingness.

I opened my eyes to find myself in the same room that I had woken up in when I attempted to escape. I figured it was the same room and there would be nothing new, but I saw a portable phone sitting on the desk next to the computer. Motorola, of course, top of the line. I picked it up and sat down, since my feet were hurting a little. I called my house number, 305-892-7842. The phone started ringing, but I got the usual "We're sorry, but the number you have reached has been disconnected or is no longer in service. If you feel you have reached this recording in error, please check the number and try your call again." I thought it made sense, because my parents never picked up calls anyway, so I laughed a little. I imagined myself back in Miami, sitting on the beach with my friends and watching the sunset as we made stupid jokes and played hacky sack. I teared up a bit but forgot about it as soon as possible because I didn't want to get my clothes all soaked in tears.

I put the phone back on the desk and walked over to the computer and mindlessly typed in "Illumini." It went to a loading screen. After recovering from being light-headed, I realized what I had done, and I stared intently at the screen. After a minute or so, it went to a command screen, so I typed in "help," and a huge list of different commands came up. I scrolled through the gargantuan list of words and descriptions and came across "end simulation." I stared at those two words for minutes, just imagining what they could mean. I decided not to type them in, since I wasn't sure what that command would do, and I left.

8
ELVIRA

I woke up back in my bed at The Keeper...same clothes, same everything, but something felt off. Was it my hair? Was it me being lightheaded? What was it? I tried to clear my head and looked around, checking everything out. I got up and opened the door, and it was then I remembered I had broken the lock before I went to the "computer room."

I used the elevator to go down to the ground floor. I left without even the receptionist noticing me. I walked down the street, hooded figures passing me without giving me a glance.

I saw a Betamax store not too far from the tower. I went inside and was greeted with teal colored walls and a sweet candy-like smell. I looked around and saw shelves upon shelves of Betamax tapes and music cassettes. I browsed around the store for a while before picking out "Airplane." I had never seen it, but I had heard it was hysterical, so I decided to buy it. Once I got up to the counter, I remembered I had no money! I didn't even know what currency they used! I started turning to put the movie back, when the cashier said I could have it for free.

"Elvira said it was alright," he said with a cheery grin.

I instantly wondered, "Who is Elvira? Is she the lady in the tower? Is she a stranger I have yet to meet?" My mind was racing from thought to thought, trying to piece it all together. I thanked the guy at the counter and went back to the tower with my movie. Back in my room, I closed the door and put the tape in, but minutes into the movie, the woman barged into my room and said she wanted to talk to me.

"Okay, just let me finish this."

"No, now," she exclaimed in an almost sneery tone of voice. I guess this might've been because I had left the tower without her knowing.

I walked out and she had me take a seat on one of the chairs in front of her desk while she sat in her chair. "Where did you go last night?" she asked.

"Nowhere, ma'am. I was lying in bed," I lied.

"That's not what I think. You're not the same person that came in here yesterday; you seem different. Somehow, in some way, you're different."

I felt a hot wave of stress cover my body and said, "Yeah, I feel different too; I must have slept weird."

She gave me a "yeah, okay sure" kind of look. I got up and started walking towards my room, but she stopped me. "Oh, and you're welcome for the free movie."

Well, now I know what her name is. "Thank you, Elvira," I said before closing my bedroom door and finishing my movie.

9
EXIT STRATEGY

I woke up the next day to the same thing as the day before--the sun rising over a metropolis. The door was unlocked, which was weird, especially considering the events of the previous days. I left the room but was greeted by the same gangsters who had held up Elvira my first night in the tower. There were three of them surrounding the door, and one of them was holding Elvira hostage. I looked at all of them quickly and asked them what they wanted. Almost immediately, the one in the middle asked me to show them "the room."

I felt a surge of adrenaline. "My room? Or the…" I paused for a moment, not wanting to say, "the other room," because that would raise suspicions, and things could get a lot, lot worse.

"The other room. Now!" the gangster said.

So they knew then. "Okay, okay, come with me and I'll show you," I said in a shaky voice. They shoved past me and forced their way into my room. I guessed they assumed the other room was in my room. "Just smash out the window and jump out and I'll show you."

"Do you really think we're THAT stupid?" one of them said.

"No, I'm being honest. I wouldn't lie to the guys with guns here." But in my mind, I was thinking, "Yes."

"Yeah, ok--" Before the gangster could finish his sentence, Elvira had him on the ground with his head turned backwards. She kicked his Uzi to me, and it slid across the floor and bumped into my foot.

"SHOOT!" she yelled.

I picked the gun up and unloaded five shots into the gangster on my right while Elvira smacked the other gangster in the back of the head with his gun. I stopped and stared in astonishment at what we had just done.

Elvira shook me back to life and said, "There are more on the way; we need to move now."

I wanted to say, "Okay, let's go," but my lips stumbled around, and I went "uhm", like an idiot.

Elvira shot out the window. "Are you sure this is the way out?"

It was weird that she trusted me enough to do this. I nodded rapidly, figuring that I shouldn't speak anymore since I'd probably sound like an idiot. She shoved me out and followed me. Before I knew it, we were both in the terminal room.

"Where are we?" Elvira asked.

I was amazed that she had no idea what this room was, especially considering she was one of the first people here. "I've been here before, but I just don't know what this room actually is. The terminal on the table there is used for giving commands to the S.M.V., and I know the password for it, that is, if you want to know it," I said.

She seemed to ignore me for a few seconds, looking around the room and inspecting the terminal, before finally turning to me and saying, "Yeah, what's the password?"

I thought for a second and then blurted out, "Illumini."

Her fingers flew across the keyboard and pressed enter. The computer went to the loading screen and Elvira stared at it intently until the command screen came up. She looked at it for a second, probably thinking about what to type in, and then typed "help." She scrolled through the list of commands and found the "end simulation" command. She scrolled past it and read the rest of the list, and then went back up to the "end simulation" command and turned to me.

"Ready?" she asked.

"Yeah, I'm ready," I said.

She clicked on it and everything went black.

10
REALITY

I awoke inside a Kritotoshi Cryo-Stasis pod. Kritotoshi was the Nami corporation's main competitor, and they specialized in biochemical research and cybernetics.

It was cold inside the pod, and there were a bunch of wires and stuff hanging off the outside from what I could see through the pod window. I felt stiff and aching all over. I shook myself to warm up and looked for a way out. My eyes crossed an emergency release lever on the ceiling of the pod. I pulled it down and it began opening slowly. Once it was fully opened, musty, old air filled the pod. I climbed out and stretched. I inspected the pod--it was old, covered in dust, and the glass was scratched and well-worn.

There were other pods like mine down the hallway. Most of them either said "compromised" or "active." I decided to try to find a way out, and I walked further down the hallway. It was silent and eerie, the lights were dim, and there was no sound other than my footsteps. I suddenly heard a loud hissing noise behind me. I stopped dead in my tracks and turned around to see one of the pods opening. I tensed a little, but still felt unnerved. I walked over at an insanely slow speed, forcing my footsteps not to give away my position. I stopped a good two meters away from the pod and waited for its inhabitant to crawl out.

I was expecting an old rotted corpse to fall out, but to my astonishment, an almost uncanny copy of Elvira came out. She fell out limp and I caught her. "How romantic," I thought. I laid her down and shook her awake.

She recovered almost immediately. "Where are we? Did we make it out?"

"Yes, this is as real as reality gets." I managed to get her up and walking and we went further down the hall. The silence was becoming more intense and a quiet awkwardness was beginning to form. I asked her about who she was and what she did before she entered the S.M.V.

"I really don't remember. I know my father was the owner of a big tech company, but I don't remember which one."

I told her about my life before the S.M.V. and she thought it was funny that I still liked cassettes. She said she listened to 8-tracks, which wasn't uncommon--they were popular.

When we found the end of the hall, we were greeted by a large metal door. It looked like it was made to withstand a nuclear blast. Maybe it was. There was a large keypad next to the door, but it seemed to have been pried off with a crowbar and was hanging on by the wires noodling into the wall.

I decided to tinker with it, since I have intermediate knowledge about circuits (not to brag, of course). I must have connected something with something that mattered because there was a violent "PSSHH" sound and then the door slowly swung open. Behind it was a longer, bunker-like hallway with a guard post. In the chair at the guard station was a skeleton wearing a Defentek uniform. Defentek was a widely known Private Military Contractor (PMC) that was famous for having the best armed and best trained security and military personnel in the world. It was considered one of the world's stronger military powers.

The bones looked burned and old, as if something very, very hot had scorched them. I turned around to see if the door was still open and I saw it was black with dust and had burn marks all over the surface. I had an idea what had caused all this, but I didn't want to confirm it, nor say it to Elvira, since I didn't want to worry her.

When we finally made it through the destroyed ruins of the bunker, a dim, gray light shone through the rubble. We looked at each other with a worried expression on our faces. What lay in front of us was what I was afraid of--a desolate wasteland. No green trees, no green grass. Only brown shrubs which had dried up, and the remains of a city in the distance.

11
THE PAINFUL TRUTH

We both stood silent at the entrance to the bunker. A warm breeze crept across our goosebump-covered skin.

I swallowed hard. "Where is everyone? What happened to this place?"

"I have no idea," Elvira said in a shaky, almost depressed voice.

I started walking towards the city that was off in the distance. I didn't ask Elvira if she wanted to come, since she seemed too caught up in the moment.

She started following me. "Where are you going? There's nothing left, no one left."

It hurt my mind to think about that, so I ignored her and kept on walking.

"WHAT DO YOU THINK WE'RE GOING TO FIND? AN ANSWER? THE TRUTH?" she yelled.

These words shoved themselves into my mind. I didn't want to listen to her anymore; I couldn't listen to her. I walked faster and her footsteps stopped doubling mine. I looked back and she was gone. At first, I thought I had found freedom from her vile words, but then I started to shake and just sat down and cried. "God, why did I get into this, why did I have to be the one to do that stupid experiment? Why? Just why…" I lay on my back and looked up to the barren sky. No sunlight shone through, there were no stars or blue skies; just clouds.

I sat back up after ten minutes and started walking again. My feet were hurting as I grew closer to the city. I felt a sense of dread when I entered the earthly necropolis, those tall, crumbling buildings towering over me. Barren shops and apartments sat silently. I felt a presence near me, as if an unearthly entity was hunting me. I turned around as fast as possible to reveal nothing out of the ordinary--just a barren, dusty street filled with the ghostly moans of the past haunting it.

I kept on walking and came across a watch shop and walked inside. I figured that if I wanted to find out what the date was, I might as well look in a place that sold devices for that. I scoured the shop and found a digital LCD Casio watch. Thanks to Nami's self-recharging batteries, it still worked. I wiped the dust off and read the date on it. 4/23/67. "No way. This watch must be broken; it can't be 2067," I thought, so I picked up another one and checked it. Same thing. I did that three more times before finally coming to the conclusion that maybe Elvira was right and nothing was left. I left and tripped over a broken newspaper vending machine. The glass was shattered, so I took a paper. The text was faded but still legible, and the date was March 23rd, 2019. "THE END," said the headline. "That's overly dramatic," I thought, trying to comfort myself with my bad sense of humor.

"The attempted peace talks with Communist Russia have failed. Despite the best efforts of the United Nation's politicians and military leaders, nuclear strikes across the U.S. and Canada are imminent. This is the end of life as we know it, ladies and gentlemen, so gather your loved ones and hold them close in our final moments. Thank you for reading, and God bless America."

I dropped the paper and slid down against the wall. "The end." Those words echoed through my mind like yelling into a canyon. I was free of all thoughts. I saw another paper next to it labeled "GORBACHEV DEAD." I picked it up and read it as well. "Mikhail Gorbachev, leader of the Soviet Socialist party, was assassinated at age 89 by U.S. special forces this morning. The assassination was planned out by James "Maddog" Mattis, and it was performed by U.S. and British forces in order to strengthen the U.S.'s grip on the Middle East." This paper had been published on March 21. It all made sense now. The U.S. had assassinated Gorbachev because things were heating up in the Middle East due to the two forces going at it for strategic military positions. The U.S. thought that, with Gorbachev dead, the USSR would fall, and the forces would either dwindle or just collapse entirely. However, the Soviet Union's leaders answered the assassination with nuclear strikes. Maybe if the Cold War had finished back in the 60s, and if democracy had managed to cause the fall of the USSR back in 1991…maybe none of this would've happened.

I didn't know where I would go from there. Back to the S.M.V.? Back to Miami, if it still even existed? I had no idea. I stood up with the little energy I had left and walked back to the bunker. I thought I would just sit there and live out the rest of my days where not even light would find me.

When I got back, I heard footsteps down the hall past the blast door. I figured it was Elvira, but when I got closer, I saw a man in a lab coat and the same two gangsters from before surrounding the scientist and Elvira. I started to creep up slowly and tried to get the jump on them. I guess they had a scout or someone out on patrol, because I heard footsteps behind me, and before I could turn to see who it was, I was smacked to the ground with a heavy blow to my back. My face hit the ground with a hard-slapping sound. I turned over on my back and saw a tall man standing over me. He grabbed me by my shirt and walked me over to the group of gangsters. He shoved me in between two of the gangsters and I fell in next to Elvira and the scientist.

Elvira looked at me and gave me a sneer. "Nice timing, don't you think?"

I gave her a "yeah, okay cool" look, but she seemed to take it as a "screw you too" kind of look. I whispered to her everything that I had found out.

"Yeah, these guys told me all about it. They said that they were a part of the Miami chapter of the Soviet mafia "D'yavol.""

"Supposedly, they were notorious and had quite an influence in Miami, so they decided to sneak into the bunker disguised as scientists in order to survive the explosions which they knew were coming. The ACTUAL scientist that's next to me, explained that this bunker was constructed in order to preserve a certain number of humans in case the bombs fell. The S.M.V. was just a front for all this. The bombs were dropped back in 2019. We have been inside the S.M.V. for 87 years, although for you and me it felt like a lot less time." Elvira told me all this in a freakishly calm tone of voice.

It all made sense now, but at the same time it didn't. Why was I chosen to be a test subject? Why was preserving humans so important? Why did all these things happen so suddenly? And how come some gangsters got a free ticket from death but I didn't have any say in surviving the bombs? I had so many questions, but I had no one to give me answers. When I turned to ask the scientist, he said that Elvira had "pretty much summed it up for me."

I asked the gangsters why they had strong-armed a floppy disc from Elvira in the S.M.V. They said that the disc held information on other mob bosses and gangs in the city. They were trying to get to the top of the criminal food chain, and in return they guarded her tower from unwanted guests. Elvira explained that she didn't want the crime rate to rise in Illumini, so the information she had given them was either faulty or outdated, and the gangsters had turned on her. I asked them what would happen next, and they were as puzzled as I was. "We have no reason to stay inside the S.M.V.; we thought that we would stay there permanently, but we'd rather live a real life than a life inside a computer. Besides, we were severely outnumbered, and we realized that, even if we had the information, we wouldn't be able to take down the other gangs. We will find a new life elsewhere."

The gangsters turned around and left. It was kind of funny--they had gone to all this trouble to just up and leave. I had no idea what they wanted to achieve. Maybe they thought the USSR was still around, or maybe they wanted to explore the ruins of America.

I asked the scientist if he could put us back into the S.M.V., and he said he could and he would, if that's what we felt we wanted. He made clear that the chances of returning from the S.M.V again were very unlikely.

Elvira and I considered our situation and decided that a life inside a world where everything was slightly normal would be better than a life in a world with nothing left. We both agreed to live out the remainders of our days inside the S.M.V.

Before the scientist put us back in, he gave Elvira a note from the CEO of Nami himself, saying that it was important and was meant to be read if or when she returned to the real world.

It read: *"Daughter Elvira, I love you very dearly, and want only the best for you. I know you may not forgive me for what I have done, but I have ensured that you will have a life beyond mine, and everyone else's. I hope you understand the circumstances of which I am writing this note to you. Sincerely, your father, Jiro Zachota."*

Elvira folded the letter and put it in her pocket, trying to hold back the tears. We climbed into the pods once again and put on helmets similar to the ones I had to wear the first time I entered the S.M.V. The scientist counted down and hit the button, and then, all of a sudden, there was a bright flash and everything went dark.

The End

ABOUT BLAKE LONGDON

So, I was born in 2003 on November 11th, (convenient date 11/11) and was raised by my two wonderful parents. I have tons of interests, mainly revolving around gaming and physical activities, I like to get out and do stuff, whether it be traveling or just going out to the store. One of my favorite things to do that actually gets me out of the house is airsoft and my friends, they motivate me to wake up every day and push through every day. Whether it be hard or easy, they're always there for me. I was encouraged by my wonderful friend Mary Dee to finish writing Retrowave 2067. It initially started as a little pet project which I did just because I love synthwave culture so much. But it soon turned into much more a year or two later. Now I'm writing this biography on myself for you to read.

Connect with Blake

Official Author Site:
http://ausxippublishing.com/authors/blake-longdon/

Official Instagram Account:
https://www.instagram.com/retrowave_2067/

ABOUT AUSXIP PUBLISHING

AUSXIP Publishing's goal is to bring you quality stories with strong characters that inspire, strengthen and enrich the soul– to build you up, to create a sense of achievement and most importantly to entertain. We love reading about characters who change their world.

All the hallmarks that made AUSXIP Network a place where people want to congregate is what we want to replicate. AUSXIP Publishing is the company that produces the books we want to read if we were not writing or publishing them ourselves. Come with us on our journey and lose yourself in our books and grow with us.

Your can find us here:

- AUSXIP Publishing – http://ausxippublishing.com
- Facebook: http://facebook.com/ausxippublishing
- Twitter: http://twitter.com/ausxippublish

www.ingramcontent.com/pod-product-compliance
Lightning Source LLC
Chambersburg PA
CBHW071137100726

47908CB00008B/2627